# Dear Parent:
## Your child's love of reading starts here!

Every child learns to read in a different way and at his or her own speed. Some go back and forth between reading levels and read favorite books again and again. Others read through each level in order. You can help your young reader improve and become more confident by encouraging his or her own interests and abilities. From books your child reads with you to the first books he or she reads alone, there are I Can Read Books for every stage of reading:

### SHARED READING
Basic language, word repetition, and whimsical illustrations, ideal for sharing with your emergent reader

### BEGINNING READING
Short sentences, familiar words, and simple concepts for children eager to read on their own

### READING WITH HELP
Engaging stories, longer sentences, and language play for developing readers

### READING ALONE
Complex plots, challenging vocabulary, and high-interest topics for the independent reader

I Can Read Books have introduced children to the joy of reading since 1957. Featuring award-winning authors and illustrators and a fabulous cast of beloved characters, I Can Read Books set the standard for beginning readers.

A lifetime of discovery begins with the magical words "I Can Read!"

*Visit www.icanread.com for information*
*on enriching your child's reading experience.*

*For my niece Ana Natalia,*
*who loves dogs and isn't afraid of*
*anything.*
*¡Te quiero!*
*—E.O.*

*To Lucio, the most wonderful dog*
*that life provided me the opportunity*
*of loving and caring for.*
*—A.L.*

I Can Read® and I Can Read Book® are trademarks of HarperCollins Publishers.

Reina Ramos Meets a BIG Puppy
Text copyright © 2023 by Emma Otheguy
Illustrations copyright © by Andrés Landazábal
All rights reserved. Printed in the United States of America.
No part of this book may be used or reproduced in any manner whatsoever without written permission except in the case of brief quotations embodied in critical articles and reviews. For information address HarperCollins Children's Books, a division of HarperCollins Publishers,
195 Broadway, New York, NY 10007.
www.icanread.com

Library of Congress Control Number: 2022946688
ISBN 978-0-06-322315-8 (trade bdg.) — ISBN 978-0-06-322313-4 (pbk.)

Book design by Elaine Lopez
23 24 25 26 27 LB 10 9 8 7 6 5 4 3 2 1    First Edition

# Reina Ramos
## Meets a BIG Puppy

by Emma Otheguy
pictures by Andrés Landazábal

**HARPER**
*An Imprint of HarperCollinsPublishers*

Saturdays are for FUN!

Lila and I go to the park.

4

We show off our gymnastics.

Lila does forward rolls,

and I practice cartwheels.

I've almost got them down!

Our neighbor Ms. Carol cheers.

She carries her tiny dog, Gala,

in her bag.

Lila and I love Gala.

While we do gymnastics,

Gala sticks her head out and yaps.

It sounds like Gala is saying

"Bravo!"

Lila brings a new sticker book

to school on Monday.

It's full of dog stickers.

"Guess what?" she says.

"I'm getting a dog!"

"Wow!" I say.

I find a sticker that looks like Gala,

and I put it on my notebook.

I can't wait to meet the dog!

I can show it my cartwheels!

I tell my whole building
about Lila's dog.
My downstairs neighbor Mr. Ortiz
even gives me a chew toy!
I bring it to the park on Saturday.

"There's Lila!" I tell Mami.

I run toward her.

Then I stop.

Lila's dad has a dog with him.

But it's nothing like Gala.

This dog is HUGE!

"Meet Chico!" Lila says.

"Want to give him the chew toy?"

asks Mami.

Then Chico barks!

I see his pointy teeth.

I shove the toy at Mami.

"¡Toma! Take it!

You give it to him.

I'm going to practice cartwheels."

I run far away from Chico,

the biggest dog ever.

Mami catches up to me.

"Reina? What's wrong?

Are you scared?"

"Of course not!" I say.

"I love dogs!"

I focus hard on trying to cartwheel.

I always go a little sideways.

I try to straighten up.

Then it happens—I do a cartwheel!

I do another, and another!

"Mami, watch!"

"¡Eso!" she says. "Great job!"

Ms. Carol hurries by.

I get ready to cartwheel.

"Look at me, Ms. Carol!" I call.

"I'll watch next time, Reina.

Today I have to run," she replies.

There's no one around to watch.

I want to show Lila.

But she's with Chico.

At school on Monday,

Lila only wants to talk about dogs.

"Look at my cartwheel,"

I say at recess.

"Cool," says Lila. "Guess what?

Chico can give me his paw."

"Want to try a cartwheel?

I bet I could help you," I say.

Lila shakes her head.

"I'll stick with forward rolls.

Did you know Chico can sit?"

I'm annoyed.

I want Lila to cartwheel with me.

When Lila's dad comes
to walk us home from school,
he's got Chico with him!
"Reina, ¡mira!" says Lila. "Look!"
Lila shows me Chico's paw.
I get as far away as I can.

Lila scrunches up her nose.

"What's wrong with you?" she asks.

I keep walking.

Ahead of us,

a pigeon hops on the sidewalk.

Chico sees it.

He tugs on his leash.

He barks so loudly I jump!

I cover my eyes and crouch down.

Lila's dad grabs Chico's leash.

Lila kneels by me.

"Are you okay?

You look scared."

"No, I don't," I say.

But I don't move either.

"It's okay to be scared," Lila says.

"I didn't know.

I thought you liked dogs."

"I like little dogs, like Gala.

I didn't know Chico would be big."

"You should have told me," says Lila.

"I thought you didn't want to play."

I uncover one eye.

"I love playing with you," I reply.

"I didn't want you to laugh at me."

"I would never laugh," Lila says.

"Want to know something?

I'm afraid of cartwheels."

"But you love gymnastics!" I say.

"I like when I'm close to the ground.

Like forward rolls. Not cartwheels."

"I'm sorry I tried to make

you cartwheel.

Next time let's say no pressure,"

I tell Lila.

"And you don't have to

play with Chico," Lila says.

When we go to the park again,
Lila plays with Chico
while I do cartwheels.
Then she gives Chico's leash
back to her dad.

We lie in the grass.

Lila is happy.

"I wish Ms. Carol was around,"
I say.

"It's fun when she watches us—
like having a real audience!"

"I have an idea!" Lila says.

She gets her dad and Chico.

"Don't worry," Lila says.

"Chico, sit!"

Chico sits, and he doesn't bark.

He doesn't seem as big now.

"¡Vamos!" Lila shouts.